THE LEGEND OF
PECOS BILL

To KATHY—

friend, wife, and mother—

unswerving devotion
through unnerving commotion

—T.S.

THE LEGEND OF PECOS BILL

A Bantam Little Rooster Book / October 1992

Little Rooster is a trademark of Bantam Books, a division of
Bantam Doubleday Dell Publishing Group, Inc.

Designed by GDS / Jeffrey L. Ward

Library of Congress Cataloging-in-Publication Data
Small, Terry.
The legend of Pecos Bill / by Terry Small.
p. cm.
''A Bantam little rooster book.''
Summary: Retells in verse the tale of the extraordinary cowboy who was
raised by coyotes, married Sluefoot Sue, and rode the wild rapscallion
mustang stallion named Widowmaker.
ISBN 0-553-07583-7
1. Pecos Bill (Legendary character)—Legends. [1. Pecos Bill (Legendary
character) 2. Folklore—United States. 3. Tall tales. 4. Stories in
rhyme.] I. Title.
PZ8.3.S63537Ld   1992
398.2—dc20
[E]   91-16063
                                                          CIP
                                                           AC

Published simultaneously in the United States and Canada

Bantam Books are published by Bantam Books, a division of Bantam Doubleday
Dell Publishing Group, Inc. Its trademark, consisting of the words ''Bantam
Books'' and the portrayal of a rooster, is Registered in U.S. Patent and Trademark
Office and in other countries. Marca Registrada. Bantam Books, 666 Fifth
Avenue, New York, New York 10103.

PRINTED IN HONG KONG
SCP   0 9 8 7 6 5 4 3 2 1

THE LEGEND OF
PECOS BILL

Written and illustrated by

Terry Small

A BANTAM LITTLE ROOSTER BOOK
NEW YORK · TORONTO · LONDON · SYDNEY · AUCKLAND

Gather round, folks; there's a tale needs tellin'
And it's time that the tale be told.
Come listen, if you will, about Pecos Bill
In the Winter of the Bone-deep Cold.

The very first words that little Bill spoke
Got froze right in front of his head.
It was late spring thaw when his ma and his pa
First heard what their baby had said.

Now the babe bounced out of the wagon back
While the family was bumpin' out west,
And a year passed by till they wondered why
There was so much room for the rest.

Little Pecos Bill joined a coyote pack
And was raised by a coyote mother.
If you think her too wild to be rearin' a child,
Well—Bill never asked for no other.

He was halfway grown when he met with a man
By the name of Bowleg Truman,
Who convinced him to look in a slow-movin' brook
And to see for himself he was human.

"You got no tail," old Bowleg says.
"But I'm crawlin' with fleas," Bill wails.
"Put your mind at ease—all Texans got fleas,
But coyotes gotta have tails."

So Pecos Bill agreed to wear clothes
And to find him a horse and a wife;
But his coyote heart made it clear from the start
He'd be lonesome the rest of his life.

His first real partner was hardly a friend,
But a beast called Judas Iscariot—
A full-blood puma he'd saddled in Yuma
And roped with a rattlesnake lariat.

It didn't work out for Judas and Bill;
They just never got too close.
They'd gripe and snivel; they only spoke civil
The mornin' they said "Adios!"

Now that was the Year of the Texas Drought,
When there wasn't a drop to spare;
When prairie-dog holes and the tunnels of moles
Were dug through the dust in the air.

All alone and dry, Bill pointed his boots
To the land where two's a crowd—
Up round Oklahoma he caught the aroma
Of rain in a cyclone cloud.

He roped that twister and cinched it up tight
And leaped on, grabbin' that tether.
The cyclone soared and hollered and roared,
Jam-packed with a load full of weather.

Bill thumbed its withers and yanked its ears
And whacked at the storm with his hat.
It shook him to shivers, tied knots in the rivers,
And trampled East Texas flat.

Outside of Laredo that rowdy tornado
Gave out and agreed to lay still:
With its spirit all broke by a lone cowpoke,
It rained out from under old Bill.

And that's when he first got a look at the horse
That fluttered his heart with love:
A wild rapscallion, mustang stallion
Racin' the storm-clouds above.

"He can't be rode," the trail boss said.
"He's a devil-whipped backbone-breaker.
So many have tried, so many have died,
We call him the Widowmaker."

Well, I reckon you guessed Bill wasn't impressed,
And I reckon you know what he done.
That mustang got busted: one rider he trusted,
And Pecos Bill was the one.

Many a time Bill warned his boys
To keep well away from his horse;
And any who tried to sneak a short ride
Ended up with a pack of remorse.

Bill loved that horse and the horse loved him
And they rode till the saddle got raw.
Then they stopped in the breeze of the cottonwood trees
By the banks of the Washitaw.

Well, by and by a catfish flopped
And it dropped and it flopped once more—
Now a Washitaw cat gets as long and as fat
As a whale off the Cape Cod shore.

So it took Bill a minute to notice the gal
Who was ridin' the back of that critter.
Her hair was all copper, her language improper;
She looked like a real go-gitter.

She clung to the fin as the fish plunged in,
Up and down like a big carousel;
And in between splashes, she batted her lashes
And hollered a good rebel yell.

Now Bill couldn't know at a casual glance
That here was a remarkable breed:
She was tough as a longhorn, lean as a pronghorn,
Squirmy as a centipede.

Her ma was a squaw of the Chickasaw nation,
Pa was a loup-garou;
And she was the kind who knew her own mind
And did what she wanted to do.

Now ain't that a gal for me, thought Bill
As he stepped from the trees all shady.
Like a true heartbreaker, he forgot Widowmaker
And he yelled to the fish-bustin' lady.

"I'm Pecos Bill—pleased to meet you, ma'am—
I'm a slap-leather buckaroo.
I'm coyote-bred and flapjack-fed
And raised on hullabaloo.

"I'm rattlesnake-quick and tumbleweed-free
And mean as the Devil below.
I'm tough as beef jerky from old Albuquerque
And pleased if you'd say hello."

The lady hauled in the Washitaw cat
And leaped to the Washitaw shore.
She eyed Bill up and she eyed him down
And she eyed him up some more.

"Hello!" she cried in a boisterous voice.
"I'm the pride of the Washitaw Valley.
I'm an unbridled filly, the hottest red chili
This side of old Mexicali.

"I've slept in the yuccas and raised quite a ruckus
And dropped every tune that I've carried.
I'm Sluefoot Sue and pleased to meet *you*,
And I reckon we ought to get married."

You may call it love, you may call it a bluff,
You may call it the stuff on your shoe;
But a genu-wine thrill latched on to Bill
At the words of Sluefoot Sue.

Now the preacher-man came on a Arkansaw mule
With a black-back Bible in hand,
And he said, "For an eagle I'll make it all legal,
In words you can both understand."

So Pecos Bill took the ten-gallon hat
From off'n his ten-gallon head,
And he stood for a while with the horse-tooth smile
Of a cowpoke about to be wed.

It was maybe an hour in the hot Texas sun,
It was maybe an hour and a half,
Till Sluefoot Sue, long overdue,
Turned his smile to a horse-tooth laugh.

She was all gussied-up in a white lace gown,
All scrubbed and pinned and flouncy—
Bill looked behind, surprised to find
New bulges, big and bouncy.

"Wipe that grin!" she huffed and scowled.
"My saddle-end's all muscle.
This here ain't real, just good spring-steel
Of a Boston whalebone bustle."

The preacher-man spoke from the back of his mule
And they mumbled their quick "I do's":
Bill's ten-dollar spurs were just like hers,
Stickin' out from her two-dollar shoes.

FIRST CHURCH OF THE STAKED PLAINS

REV. MORDECAI SOULRUSTLER, D.D., D.D.S.

NO SIDEWINDERS, DESPERADOS, OR OTHER ORNERY VARMINTS

NUPTIAL PARAPHERNALIA AND ACCOUTREMENTS

Then Pecos Bill sidled up to Sue
And he planted a kiss on his bride.
She allowed him to hold her, peerin' over his shoulder
At the horse only one man could ride.

Then quick as a flash she was off at a dash
And she leaped with a swish and a rustle!
She landed a-straddle Widowmaker's saddle
In her dress and her spurs and her bustle.

"Yippee-yi-ti-yay!" she was heard to say.
"Ain't no critter ole Sue can't bust!"
Then they lit out alone leavin' Bill on his own
With a mouth full of prairie dust.

Widowmaker reared like a horse gone mad.
He pinwheeled, dodged, and dipped;
He just didn't know her—determined to throw her,
He ducked and he bucked and backflipped.

Now Sluefoot Sue hung tight like a tick,
And it looked like she'd bust him soon.
But she ran out of luck when she had to duck
From bumpin' her head on the moon.

Then she lost her grip and she started to slip,
And she tumbled back over the tail.
Bill watched her fallin' with arms and legs sprawlin'
And weddin' dress spread like a sail.

She hit that prairie like a lightning bolt
Smack-dab on her bustled behind,
And the spring-steel coil bounced her up from the soil
To the place where the zodiac shined.

This time the moon had to dodge a piece,
Till gravity yanked her down,
But she sprung back up to the Big Dipper's cup
Like a cannon-shot circus clown.

First up and then down went Sluefoot Sue,
The bouncin' bride of the prairie.
For forty-two days Bill shouted the praise
Of his high-flyin' spring canary.

"I'm plumb out of grub!" she hollered at last,
"And I don't mean salads and greens!"
So every new moon Bill set out a spoon
With a pan full of refried beans.

Now I ain't actually factually sure
What happened right after that;
But I heard it from Bill that she's bouncin' still,
Only gettin' prodigiously fat.

And Widowmaker left with his dander up
That Bill gave his heart to another;
And now Bill prowls with occasional howls
For his horse and his gal and his mother.

You can hear him wail at the end of the trail
Where good friends drift apart.
If it sounds all throaty, it's no coyote,
Just Bill with a lonesome heart.